趣味漫畫學英語

小學漫畫英語王

Collocations
字詞搭配

Aman Chiu 著

新雅文化事業有限公司
www.sunya.com.hk

想英語更地道？
從字詞搭配（Collocations）入手！

本書主題

全書以字詞搭配為主題，共有60個單元，囊括小學生常用的500多組英語字詞搭配，內容豐富實用，形式生動有趣，有助提升英語水平！

漫畫看一看

每個單元用趣味漫畫講解一組重點字詞搭配，孩子可輕鬆辨別正確和錯誤的用法，增添學習樂趣。

字詞搭配你要知

全面解說小學生必學的字詞搭配知識，包括 4 個欄目：

1. 地道英語這樣說
2. 實用例句齊來學
3. 字詞搭配加分站
4. 增潤知識大放送

❶ 🔊 地道英語這樣說

針對小學生常犯錯誤，說明地道英語的字詞搭配組合，輕鬆踢走中式英語和母語干擾的問題。

❷ ★ 實用例句齊來學

收錄雙語例句，示範詞彙最自然的使用情況，讀者可先消化學習，後模仿應用。

❸ 字詞搭配加分站

提供大量與重點詞目相關的字詞搭配，建立孩子的英文詞彙量，提升寫作能力。

❹ 🔍 增潤知識大放送

一網打盡文法、語法、特殊用法等增潤內容，從小培養孩子的英文語感。

字詞搭配你要知

🔊 地道英語這樣說
在中文裏，我們會說「造成破壞或損失」，但英文沒有 make damage 這個說法。要表達上述意思，damage 主要有兩個動詞可搭配，分別是 do 和 cause。

★ 實用例句齊來學
- Too much sunlight can do serious damage to your skin.
  過猛的陽光會對皮膚造成嚴重傷害。
- This scandal will do a lot of damage to his reputation.
  這宗醜聞將大大損害他的聲譽。
- The storm caused serious damage to the crops.
  暴風雨對農作物造成了嚴重破壞。
- The explosion caused over \$500,000 worth of damage.
  爆炸造成了價值逾 50 萬元的損失。

字詞搭配加分站
slight damage 輕微的損壞
- The temple suffered slight damage by fire.
  火災令這座廟宇遭受輕微的損毀。
widespread damage 大規模的破壞
- The earthquake caused widespread damage to the city.
  地震對城市造成大規模的破壞。

🔍 增潤知識大放送
damage 除了作名詞用，也可作及物動詞用，例如：
- Smoking can damage your health. 吸煙危害健康。
- The church was seriously damaged by the explosion.
  爆炸造成教堂嚴重損毀。

練習室

末附設6個練習，蓋書中所學，動動筋，鞏固知識，自檢測學習成果。

練習室 1 🏆

Choose the correct verb for the following sentences. Tick the correct box .
請為下列句子選出正確的動詞，並在 □ 加 ✓。

範例　Let's (☐ A. open　☑ B. throw　☐ C. work) a party.

❶ The earthquake (☐ A. made　☐ B. did　☐ C. formed) widespread damage to the village.

❷ I like to sit down and (☐ A. do　☐ B. play　☐ C. work out) the crossword.

❸ I really enjoy (☐ A. doing　☐ B. having　☐ C. working) exercise every day.

❹ Mary wants to (☐ A. take up　☐ B. study　☐ C. do) a course in Maths.

❺ My father (☐ A. infects　☐ B. has　☐ C. catches) a backache so he couldn't sleep well.

❻ Only 40% of the students who (☐ A. had　☐ B. joined　☐ C. took) the final exam passed it.

❼ His misbehaviour has (☐ A. arisen　☐ B. caused　☐ C. appeared) us too many problems.

❽ David seems to (☐ A. catch　☐ B. infect　☐ C. suffer) the flu every winter.

❾ He fell asleep and (☐ A. made　☐ B. had　☐ C. thought) strange dreams.

❿ He is a young man of (☐ A. big　☐ B. strong　☐ C. great) ability.

參考答案：1.B 2.A 3.A 4.C 5.B 6.C 7.B 8.A 9.B 10.C

練習室 2 🏆

What's the opposite of the following words in bold? Write the answer in the spaces provided.
以下粗體字的相反詞是什麼？請在橫線上填寫答案。

範例　There is a light wind blowing.　　strong

❶ I lost the game.

❷ Have you unpacked your suitcase yet?

❸ She is a heavy smoker.

❹ The little girl can do up her shoelaces.

❺ Fasten your seat belt now.

❻ Our work is ahead of schedule.

❼ We had heavy rain the whole evening.

❽ Hang up the phone.

❾ Chloe got very good marks in reading.

❿ He has a broad knowledge of world history.

參考答案：1. won 2. packed 3. light 4. undo 5. unfasten 6. behind 7. light 8. pick up 9. poor 10. narrow

作者的話

　　英語字詞搭配是衡量人們英語水平的一個重要指標。然而，對於華語學生而言，包括香港的學生，它卻是一道學習難關，也是讓英語水平停滯不前的無形障礙。

　　例如，中文裏說的「一羣牛」、「一羣狼」、「一羣獅子」、「一羣鴿子」、「一羣蜜蜂」、「一羣鯨魚」等，同樣都是「一羣」動物，為什麼換成英語時會變成 a herd of cattle、a pack of wolves、a pride of lions、a flock of doves、a swarm of bees 和 a school of whales？又例如，為什麼我們會寫出像 She met an accident. 或 Students can enjoy a discount. 諸如此類字詞搭配錯誤的句子？

　　很多時候，我們努力翻查詞典嘗試找出答案，也是於事無補，因為很多詞典根本沒有提供這方面的訊息。我們極其量也只能從個別例句中忖測詞語之間的組合關係，但這個學習機遇可遇不可求，猶如瞎子摸象。

　　在苦無對策之下，以前我們或會只憑感覺含糊其辭。但自從語言資料庫 (corpus) 誕生，我們便有了可靠的憑證。語言資料庫包羅了豐富而珍貴的語料，把人們自然而然又自發使用語言的情景記錄下來，反映真實的語言習慣。以前我們不能確定的問題，現在可以迎刃而解了。

　　如上述提及的 meet an accident 和 enjoy a discount，在英國國家語料庫 (British National Corpus) 中的出現次數為零。這讓我們可以肯定地說，以上兩個搭配是不恰當的。孰是孰非，一目了然，不再含混。

　　根據這樣嚴謹的方法來撰寫英語學習圖書，一來摒除以往過於人為的 (artificial) 編撰，二來讓圖書內容更如實地反映語言狀況，有助提升孩子的英語流暢程度 (proficiency)。本書便是以這個新的角度來編寫，希望對大家有用。以下為本書的四大特色：

　　第一，本書針對小學生常犯的字詞搭配錯誤而編寫，旨在提升學童的整體英語水平。

　　第二，全書共 60 課，收錄了最常見和最有用的 500 多組英語字詞搭配，同時分析學童經常犯下的母語干擾問題，以幫助他們矯正中式英語。

　　第三，書中提供大量的生活情景實用例句，展示了詞彙最地道和最自然的使用情況，讓學童在語境中理解其用法和含義，並自行模仿應用。

　　第四，書末附設 6 個練習，供自測水平，並鞏固所學。

　　最後，祝大家有一趟愉快的學習旅程！

Aman Chiu

字詞搭配是什麼？
What are collocations?

　　所謂字詞搭配，是指語言中某些字彙合併的組合，可以產生自然的口語和文字。英文字彙組合的方式雖然不全是任意，但很多用法幾乎沒有道理可言，因為這是文字長久以來的用法。例如，「濃茶」的英文是 strong tea，不是 thick tea；「紅茶」的英文是 black tea，不是 red tea；意指冷門人選的「黑馬」的英文是 dark horse，不是 black horse。這些搭配組合早已在英語演化過程中沉澱下來，成為了語言上約定俗成的用法。

　　一般而言，我們對母語的字詞搭配已習慣成自然，無須多加思索就可組成合乎語感的文句，但對英語字彙的使用，則常是費盡心思卻收效欠佳。在此情況，字典所能提供的助益就很有限。

　　舉例說，我們查字典可知道，英文可以用 heavy 來形容 rain，意思是「大雨」。可是，要表達「大風」時，就不能用 heavy wind，只能用 strong wind。相對的，表達「大雨」時，不能說 strong rain。如果硬要說 heavy wind 或 strong rain，那就顯得很不自然了。又例如，在中文，我們會說「吃藥」，但當我們生搬硬套，用英文把它說成 eat medicine，那便大錯特錯。在英語，比較自然的說法是 take medicine。

　　學習字詞搭配不難，最重要的是多看多熟悉。我們在學習單字時，可以一併了解單字與其他字詞如何組合，單字在例句中如何發揮作用，使自己沉浸在英語環境中，逐漸習得字詞的搭配關係，遠離母語干擾，同時知曉英語母語人士偏好的用法。久而久之，英語能力必定能大大提升。

目錄 Contents

✓ great musical ability
✗ high musical ability

漫畫看一看

字詞搭配你要知

◀)) 地道英語這樣說

當 ability 指「學習能力、效率」時，便可用 high 和 low 來搭配，例如：a child of high / low ability（學習能力高 / 低的孩子）。

但當 ability 所指的是「處世技巧、辦事能力等各方面的才能」時，我們就要用 great（強的）、outstanding（卓越的）或 remarkable（傑出的）等字眼。

★ 實用例句齊來學

- He is a young man of **great musical ability**.
  他是一個很有音樂才華的年青人。
- She has got **outstanding artistic ability**. 她擁有傑出的藝術才能。
- Mary has demonstrated a **remarkable ability** to get things done. 瑪莉展示了非凡的辦事能力。

字詞搭配加分站

extraordinary / exceptional abilities 非凡的才幹

- Students with **extraordinary / exceptional learning abilities** often perform better in class.
  具有非凡學習能力的學生通常在課堂上表現得較好。

natural ability 天生的能力

- He's never learnt to draw, but he has a **natural ability**.
  他從來沒有學過畫畫，但他天生就有這本領。

○ 增潤知識大放送

如表示「有能力做某事」，我們一般會説 have the ability to do something，例如：

- Bill **has the ability** to motivate people. 比爾很會激勵別人。

✔ have an accident
✘ meet an accident

漫畫看一看

Why were you late?

We met an accident on the way.

My Name is Accident!

Accident

No! We had an accident! A car accident!

Pardon? You met a friend called Accident?

Oh, no! I'm sorry to hear that.

🔊 地道英語這樣說

雖然 meet 有「遇到」的意思，但是在英語中不能説 meet an accident。

如要表達「遭遇某事情，尤其是不愉快的事」，我們會用 meet with，例如：We met with some difficulties.（我們遇到了一些困難。）所以，「遇上意外」該説成 meet with an accident。然而，更常見的搭配是 have an accident。

⭐ 實用例句齊來學

- We **met with a car accident** on our way back.
  我們回程時發生了車禍。

- John **had an accident** and was unable to go to school.
  約翰遇上意外，無法回校上課。

💣 字詞搭配加分站

suffer an accident 遭遇意外
- She **suffered a serious accident** and lost one leg.
  她遭遇嚴重意外，失去了一條腿。

in an accident 在意外中
- The old man was injured **in a traffic accident**.
  那個老人在交通意外中受傷了。

avoid / prevent an accident 避免 / 防止意外
- Wear your seat belt to **avoid / prevent an accident**.
  繫好安全帶，以防意外發生。

🔍 增潤知識大放送

have an accident 不能用於進行式或被動語態，例如我們不能說 He is having an accident. / The accident was had by him.

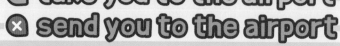
漫畫看一看

I'm going to send my cousin to the airport.

Seriously? I can't imagine putting your cousin in a big parcel and posting it off!

What?

Oh, I get it. You mean taking your cousin to the airport, right?

字詞搭配你要知

🔊 地道英語這樣說

如要表達「送某人去機場」，我們一般用 take someone to the airport。

如想強調「陪伴」的意思，可以説 accompany someone to the airport。

但純粹是「送機」的話，説 see someone off at the airport 就可以了。

★ 實用例句齊來學

- I am **taking** my Korean friends **to the airport**.
  我送我的韓國朋友去機場。

- I **accompanied** my grandparents **to the airport** last night.
  我昨晚陪同祖父母一起去機場。

- I'll **see** my friends **off at the airport** tomorrow morning.
  我明天早上會去機場送朋友機。

💬 字詞搭配加分站

drive someone to the airport 開車送……去機場

- Dad is going to **drive** them **to the airport**.
  爸爸會開車送他們去機場。

arrive at the airport 到達機場

- We **arrived at the airport** at midnight.
  我們深夜時分到達機場。

🔍 增潤知識大放送

在 take someone to the airport，動詞 take 不能隨便換成 bring，因為在 I am bringing my friends to the airport. 這句，bring 意味着「把朋友帶到機場」，而不是「送機」。

漫畫看一看

Put on a helmet when you sit on your bike.

What's the point of putting on a helmet when sitting on my bike?

It's for the sake of your safety.

Mommy, do you mean putting on a helmet while riding on my bike?

🔊 地道英語這樣說

sit on a bicycle 純粹指「坐在單車上」。我們騎單車時，可以有兩個身分，第一個是我們自己駕駛單車，身分是司機；第二個是我們乘坐單車，身分是乘客。如果想表達是司機，可以說 ride a bicycle。如果想說是乘客，則是 ride on someone's bicycle。

⭐ 實用例句齊來學

- Peter learnt to **ride a bike** when he was three.
  彼得三歲時學會了騎單車。
- It's dangerous to **ride on a bicycle** with a stranger.
  坐上陌生人的單車，是很危險的。

💡 字詞搭配加分站

get on / mount a bicycle 騎上單車
- She **got on / mounted** her **bicycle** and rode off.
  她騎上單車走了。

get off a bicycle 下單車
- **Get off** your **bicycle**. It's your sister's turn now.
  下單車吧，到你妹妹騎了。

come off / fall off a bicycle 摔下單車
- Tom **came off / fell off** his **bicycle** when it skidded on ice.
  湯姆的單車在冰上滑倒，把他摔了下來。

🔍 增潤知識大放送

在口語，一般說 bike，而不說 bicycle。

我們可用短語 by bicycle 來指「騎單車」，例如：
- I go to school **by bicycle**. 我騎單車去上學。

字詞搭配你要知

🔊 地道英語這樣說

「洗碗」是日常家務，包括清洗所有餐具，除了碗，還有碟、筷子、刀叉等，我們不能執着於一個「碗」字。

如要表達「洗碗」的意思，英文的説法是 do the dishes，也可説作 clean / wash the dishes。

⭐ 實用例句齊來學

- Whose turn to **do the dishes**? 輪到誰洗碗？

- Let me help you **do the dishes** after dinner.
  晚飯後我來幫你洗碗吧。

- Let's **clean the dishes** together. 我們一起洗碗吧。

- Have you **washed the dishes**? 你洗了碗沒有？

💡 字詞搭配加分站

dry the dishes 擦乾餐具

- David always helps **dry the dishes**. 大衛經常幫忙擦乾餐具。

put away the dishes 收起餐具

- Can you **put away the dishes**, please? 你可以把餐具收起嗎？

unwashed dishes 未洗的餐具

- Leaving **unwashed dishes** overnight can breed bacteria.
  把未洗的餐具放過夜會滋生細菌。

🔍 增潤知識大放送

dishes 作複數名詞用，必須加上定冠詞 the，即 the dishes，泛指所有餐具。

在 do the dishes，do 這個動詞包含了「清潔」的意思，其他相似的例子有 do the laundry（洗衣服）。

✓ catch a cold
✗ obtain a cold

字詞搭配你要知

🔊 地道英語這樣說

在英語，任何病都可以用 have 來搭配。

如要表示「患上感冒」，可說 have a cold 或 have got a cold［英式英語］。除此之外，人們也常說 catch a cold 或 suffer from a cold 來表達類近的意思。

⭐ 實用例句齊來學

- Don't come near me. I **got a cold**. 別靠近我，我得了感冒。
- I must have **caught a cold** in the library.
  我一定是在圖書館得了感冒。

💡 字詞搭配加分站

a bit of a cold 有點感冒
- I have **a bit of a cold** today. 我今天有點感冒。

mild / slight cold 輕微感冒
- It's a **mild / slight cold**. Don't worry. 感冒很輕微，不用擔心。

bad / heavy / nasty cold 重感冒
- John suffers from a **bad / heavy / nasty cold**. 約翰患了重感冒。

nurse a cold 調理感冒
- Mum stayed at home because she was **nursing a cold**.
  媽媽正調理感冒，所以留在家中。

🔍 增潤知識大放送

cold 作「感冒」解時，一般要加上不定冠詞 a，例如：
- Have you **got a cold**? 你患了感冒？

如果是說 flu（流感），則要加上定冠詞 the，例如：
- Have you **got the flu**? 你患了流感？

✓ a powerful computer
✗ a strong computer

字詞搭配你要知

🔊 地道英語這樣說

在英語，powerful 和 strong 是同義詞，但側重點不同。

strong 強調的是身體有力強壯，後來才引伸出強大的意思，較多用於形容人。powerful 則傾向強調權力和影響力，除了用於人外，更多用來形容 machine（機器）、engine（引擎）、weapon（武器）或 electric current（電流）等。所以，我們一般會說 a powerful computer。

⭐ 實用例句齊來學

- This is so far the most **powerful computer** in the world.
  這是目前全球功能最強的電腦。

- Nuclear bombs are more **powerful** than guns.
  核彈比槍械擁有更強大的威力。

💡 字詞搭配加分站

high-speed computer 快速的電腦
- They need a **high-speed computer** to complete that difficult task. 他們需要一部快速的電腦來完成那項困難的工作。

sophisticated computer 先進的電腦
- This **computer** is too **sophisticated** for the elderly.
  這部電腦對於長者來說太先進了。

🔍 增潤知識大放送

有些情況 powerful 與 strong 同義，例如：powerful muscles 或 strong muscles 都指強而有力的肌肉；strong smell 和 powerful smell 都指濃烈的氣味。有時兩者更會連在一起使用，例如：

- I feel **strong** and **powerful**!
  我感到精力充沛，充滿力量！

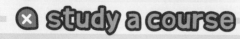

字詞搭配你要知

🔊 地道英語這樣說

我們只能用 do / take a course 來指「修讀課程」，不能說 study a course。do a course 主要用於英式英語，take a course 則用於美式英語。

⭐ 實用例句齊來學

- What type of **course** should I **do**? 我該選讀哪一種課程？
- Should I **do** an arts or science **course**? 我該選修文科還是理科呢？
- She **took a course** in Korean. 她修讀了韓文課程。

📢 字詞搭配加分站

sign up for a coure 報讀課程
- Bill has **signed up for a course** in design.
  比爾報讀了一門設計課程。

drop out of a coure 退修課程
- Why did you **drop out of the course**? 你為什麼中途退修這門課？

complete a course 修讀完課程
- I will **complete the course** this summer.
  我將會在夏天修讀完這門課。

pass a course 通過課程考試
- It is difficult to **pass the course**.
  要通過這門課的考試並不容易。

fail a course 不通過課程考試
- No one **failed the course**. 沒有人不通過課程考試。

🔍 增潤知識大放送

study 有「攻讀」的意思，作及物動詞用，須後接一門學科，例如：
- Why do we **study history / science**? 我們為何要研究歷史 / 科學？

cause damage
make damage

字詞搭配你要知

🔊 地道英語這樣說

在中文裏，我們會說「造成破壞或損失」，但英文沒有 make damage 這個說法。要表達上述意思，damage 主要有兩個動詞可搭配，分別是 do 和 cause。

⭐ 實用例句齊來學

- Too much sunlight can **do** serious **damage** to your skin.
  過猛的陽光會對皮膚造成嚴重傷害。

- This scandal will **do** a lot of **damage** to his reputation.
  這宗醜聞將大大損害他的聲譽。

- The storm **caused** serious **damage** to the crops.
  暴風雨對農作物造成了嚴重破壞。

- The explosion **caused** over $500,000 worth of **damage**.
  爆炸造成了價值逾 50 萬元的損失。

💡 字詞搭配加分站

slight damage 輕微的損壞
- The temple suffered **slight damage** by fire.
  火災令這座廟宇遭受輕微的損毀。

widespread damage 大規模的破壞
- The earthquake caused **widespread damage** to the city.
  地震對城市造成大規模的破壞。

🔍 增潤知識大放送

damage 除了作名詞用，也可作及物動詞用，例如：

- Smoking can **damage** your health. 吸煙危害健康。

- The church was seriously **damaged** by the explosion.
  爆炸造成教堂嚴重損毀。

漫畫看一看

字詞搭配你要知

🔊 地道英語這樣說

determination 指「決心」。英語有很多表示「決心很大」的説法，當中 great determination 是最常見的搭配。除此之外，還有 strong (堅定的)、grim (堅持不懈的)、dogged (頑強的) 等，都可以和 determination 搭配。

⭐ 實用例句齊來學

- She has shown **great / strong determination** and skill.
  她展示了堅定的決心和出色的技能。

- She hung on with **grim determination**.
  她以堅韌不拔的毅力堅持着。

- We succeeded through **dogged determination** plus a bit of good luck. 憑着頑強的決心和一點運氣，我們成功了。

💡 字詞搭配加分站

fierce determination 堅定不移的決心

- She is a woman of **fierce determination**.
  她有一顆堅定不移的決心。

steely determination 鋼鐵般的意志

- His **steely determination** convinced us that he was perfect for the job. 他鋼鐵般的意志，讓我們相信他能勝任這份工作。

full of determination 充滿決心

- The team is **full of determination** to win.
  這支球隊對取勝充滿決心。

🔍 增潤知識大放送

determination 的形容詞是 determined，指「堅決的」，例如：

- She's a very **determined** woman. 她是一個意志堅強的女士。

漫畫看一看

30

字詞搭配你要知

🔊 地道英語這樣說

check 指「檢查」，check a dictionary 便是「檢查詞典」，例如看看詞典有否破損，是否需要買一本新的來替換。

要表示「用字典查某單詞」，我們會說 look up a word in a dictionary，或簡短一些，refer to / consult a dictionary。

⭐ 實用例句齊來學

- I **look up** the spelling of words **in the dictionary** when writing compositions. 寫作時，我會翻查字典，找出字詞的拼寫。

- Let me **refer to** my **dictionary**. 讓我查閱一下詞典。

- Why don't you **consult a dictionary**? 你為什麼不翻查詞典？

- She **consulted** her **dictionary** to look up the meaning of the word 'encyclopaedia'.
  她查字典找出 encyclopaedia（百科全書）這個詞語的意思。

🏷 字詞搭配加分站

bilingual dictionary 雙語詞典
- An English-Chinese **bilingual dictionary** is a must-have item for students. 英漢雙解詞典是學生的必備物品。

online dictionary 網上詞典
- **Online dictionaries** always come with audio pronunciation.
  網上詞典通常會提供詞語發音。

🔍 增潤知識大放送

look up the dictionary 並不解作「查字典」。雖然 look up 有「查找」的意思，特別指從參考書把資料查找出來，但是它後面所接的賓語不能是 dictionary，而要是 word。這是因為要查找的是某字的意思，而不是詞典。

漫畫看一看

32

字詞搭配你要知

🔊 地道英語這樣說

中文裏，我們可以說「我對你徹底失望」。但在英語，人們不會說 I'm completely / totally disappointed in you. 如果想加強 disappointed 的詞義，可以用副詞 very、really、greatly、deeply、terribly 等來搭配。

⭐ 實用例句齊來學

- We were **very / really disappointed** that the other side had won. 對方獲勝，使我們非常失望。

- I was **greatly disappointed** to find the museum closed. 發現博物館關門了，我十分失望。

- We're **deeply disappointed** about the result. 我們對結果非常失望。

- He was **terribly disappointed** to learn that he had failed the course. 得知這門課不及格時，他十分失望。

🔔 字詞搭配加分站

a bit disappointed 有點失望

- She got **a bit disappointed** when she heard the news. 她聽到消息時有點失望。

bitterly disappointed 極其失望

- We're **bitterly disappointed** with the court's judgment. 我們對法庭的判決極其失望。

🔍 增潤知識大放送

同樣是形容詞，disappointed 用來指人，disappointing 則用來指事物，例如：

- What a **disappointing** performance! 這個演出太讓人失望了！

33

字詞搭配你要知

🔊 地道英語這樣說

在英語，我們可以説 enjoy a meal（享用一餐）、enjoy a film（享受看電影的樂趣）、enjoy good health（擁有健康的身體），甚或 enjoy yourself（過得快活），但不能 enjoy a discount。

英語有三個動詞經常與 discount 搭配，它們是 get、obtain 和 receive，都有「獲享折扣」的意思。

⭐ 實用例句齊來學

- The staff at the shop **get a discount** of 40%.
  商店員工可享六折購物優惠。

- To **obtain** this **discount**, one must present a student card.
  必須出示學生證，方可享這個折扣優惠。

- If you buy more than a certain amount, you will **receive a discount**. 購物超過指定金額，可享折扣優惠。

💡 字詞搭配加分站

get a 10% / 20% / 30% discount 享九折 / 八折 / 七折優惠

- Members **get a 10% / 20% / 30% discount**.
  會員可享九 / 八 / 七折優惠。

give someone a discount 給（某人）折扣

- This VIP pass **gives** you **a discount** on rail travel.
  持這張貴賓證，坐火車可享折扣。

be qualified for / entitled to a discount 合資格享折扣優惠

- If you collect 100 bonus points, you **are qualified for / entitled to a discount**. 集齊 100 分，可享折扣優惠。

🔍 增潤知識大放送

我們也可用短語 at a discount 來表示「獲享折扣」，例如：

- Employees can buy books **at a discount**. 員工購書可獲享折扣。

✔ get a disease
✘ infect a disease

字詞搭配你要知

◀)) 地道英語這樣說

如要表示「生病」，一般用 have a disease 就可以，英式英語則可用 have got a disease。

如想說「染病」，我們可用 get / catch a disease。在正式場合則可用 contract a disease。

★ 實用例句齊來學

- How long has granny **had the disease**? 祖母得這個病多久了？

- He **got** a serious lung **disease** two years ago.
  他兩年前患上嚴重的肺病。

- Lily **caught the disease** while travelling in India.
  莉莉在印度旅行時染上了這個疾病。

- One-tenth of the population has **contracted the disease**.
  已有十分之一的人口染上了這個疾病。

字詞搭配加分站

curse a disease 治癒疾病

- No one can **cure** this **disease** – it is fatal.
  沒有人能治癒這種病，它是不治之症。

spread a disease 散播疾病

- This **disease** can **spread** from person to person in several ways. 這種病可以透過不同途徑在人羣中散播開去。

suffer from a disease 患病；受疾病折磨

- She **suffered from** a rare heart **disease**. 她患上了罕見的心臟病。

◯ 增潤知識大放送

表達「某人生病了」時，我們不會用被動語態，例如我們不能說 The disease was got / caught by him.

✓ go "woof, woof"
✗ shout "wang, wang"

漫畫看一看

Do you know that animals make different sound?

Yes! A cow goes "moo" and a cat goes "meow".

A dog shouts "wang, wang"!

No! Dogs don't speak. They go "woof, woof".

🔊 地道英語這樣說

同樣的動物叫聲，不同國家的人會有不同聯想，因此就出現了不同的象聲詞。例如，中文裏我們會説「狗汪汪叫」，但是如果直接把「汪汪」翻譯成 wang wang，外國人便會一頭霧水。

在英語，形容狗吠的象聲詞是 woof 和 bow-wow，例如我們説 A dog goes 'woof, woof'. 不説 A dog shouts 'wang, wang'. 而最常用來表達「狗吠」的動詞則是 bark。

⭐ 實用例句齊來學

- "Woof, woof," went the dog. 「汪汪！」狗叫了起來。

- A cat goes "meow" and a dog goes "bow-wow".
  貓喵喵叫，狗汪汪叫。

- The dogs are barking at the strangers. 那些狗對着陌生人吠叫。

🔖 字詞搭配加分站

snarl 露出牙齒低聲吼叫

- The dog snarled at me. 這隻狗對着我齜牙低吼。

whin 哀鳴

- That poor dog is whining behind the door.
  那隻可憐的狗在門後哀鳴。

yelp 尖叫；大叫

- The dog ran up and down, yelping. 那隻狗跑來跑去，尖叫不停。

howl 嚎叫

- The injured dog was howling in pain. 那隻受傷的狗痛苦地嚎叫着。

🔍 增潤知識大放送

象聲詞 woof 和 bow-wow 屬於名詞，多數用於兒語中。

🔊 地道英語這樣說

在聚會結束時，主人很多時都會陪客人走到門口，然後說再見。在這個場合，我們不用 send 來表達，例如我們不會說 send someone to the door，而說 walk someone out 或 see / walk / show someone to the door。

⭐ 實用例句齊來學

- I'll **walk** you **out**. 我送你出去。

- She **saw / walked** me **to the door**, but she wouldn't let me go. 她把我送到門口，但不讓我走。

- After we finished our talk, she **showed** me **to the door**. 我們聊完後，她送我到門口。

💡 字詞搭配加分站

walk with someone part of the way 送某人走一段路
- Let me **walk with** you **part of the way**. 我陪你走一段路吧。

walk with someone as far as... 把某人送到某個地點
- I'll **walk with** you **as far as** the bus stop. 我送你到巴士站。

🔍 增潤知識大放送

有時候熱情的主人甚至會陪客人一起走路回家，在這個情況，我們可以這樣說 I will walk you back. / I will accompany you home. / I will walk you over to your place.

不要把 show someone to the door 說成 show someone the door（叫某人滾出去），兩者意思完全不同。

have a dream
make a dream

字詞搭配你要知

🔊 地道英語這樣說

中文裏，我們會說「做夢」，但英文不會說 make a dream，而是說 have a dream。同樣，「做噩夢」也不是 make a nightmare，而是 have a nightmare。

★ 實用例句齊來學

- I **had** a strange **dream** last night – you and I were in a desert.
  我昨晚做了一個怪夢，我和你身處在沙漠裏。

- Years after the accident I still **have nightmares** about it.
  意外發生多年，我還在做噩夢。

💣 字詞搭配加分站

achieve a dream 實現夢想

- She **achieved** her **dream** through hard work.
  她經過多番努力實現夢想。

interpret a dream 解夢

- How would you **interpret** my **dream**?
  你會如何解讀我的夢境？

a dream comes true 夢想成真

- His **dream** to become a singer **comes true**.
  他成為歌手的夢想成真了。

🔍 增潤知識大放送

have a dream about something 指「做了關於……的夢」，例如：

- I **had** a weird **dream about** fairies last night.
  昨晚我夢見仙子，真是個怪夢。

dream 可作動詞用，例如：

- I often **dream** of flying.
  我經常夢見自己在飛。

✓ take the exam
✗ join the exam

🔊 地道英語這樣說

「參加考試」最常見的英語說法是 take an examination。另外，有不少人會說 sit an exam，這個說法多用於英式英語，特別用來指參加筆試，因為考試通常都是坐着來應考的。

口語中，我們經常也會聽到 do an exam，同樣指「參加考試」。

★ 實用例句齊來學

- I failed my **exams** and I have to **take** them again.
  我考試不及格，不得不重考。

- After the holidays, we'll be **sitting the exam**.
  假期後我們就要考試了。

- Shall I **do the exam** when I don't know anything?
  我什麼都不懂，還要不要去參加考試？

🔖 字詞搭配加分站

enter for an exam 報名參加考試
- Students may **enter for** both **exams**. 學生可報名參加這兩項考試。

study for an exam 為考試而溫習
- Everyone is **studying for the exam**. 每個人都在為考試而溫習。

pass an exam 考試及格
- Did you **pass the exam**? 你考試及格嗎？

fail an exam 考試不及格
- John **failed the exam** twice. 約翰兩次考試都不及格。

do well in an exam 考試考得好
- Lily **did well in the exam**. 莉莉考試考得很好。

🔍 增潤知識大放送

examination 是正式說法，多用於書面語，人們口頭上多說 exam。

✓ give an example
✗ raise an example

漫畫看一看

The buffet is great! I ate a lot of special food.

Can you raise an example?

What are you doing?

You asked me to raise an example, and here it is! I'm just giving you an example.

字詞搭配你要知

🔊 地道英語這樣說

raise 指「舉起」，邏輯上舉起來的東西必須是實物，例如：raise your hands（舉起雙手）。raise 也可指「增加、提高」，而增加或提高的東西必須是可以量度的，例如：speed（速度）、temperature（溫度）、rent（租金）、pay（工資）等。因此，「舉例」不能說成 raise an example。

在英語，常與 example 搭配的動詞是 take、give 和 provide。

⭐ 實用例句齊來學

- Let's **take an example**. 我們舉個例子吧。

- Let me **give** you a few **examples** of what I mean.
  讓我舉幾個例子來說明我的意思。

- Could you **provide** us with some **examples**?
  你可以給我們舉幾個例子嗎？

🔦 字詞搭配加分站

use an example 運用例子

- She **used** several **examples** to illustrate her points.
  她用了幾個例子來說明自己的觀點。

draw an example 引用例子

- He illustrates his point with **examples drawn** from a report.
  他引用報告中的例子來闡釋他的觀點。

cite an example 援引實例

- Talking about international cities, the author **cited the example** of Hong Kong. 談到國際城市，作者舉了香港作為例子。

🔍 增潤知識大放送

人們常用 for example 來舉例，例如：

- George, **for example**, is a good student. 譬如說，喬治是好學生。

漫畫看一看

字詞搭配你要知

🔊 地道英語這樣說

要表示「做運動」，我們不會說 have exercise，而是說 do exercise 或 take exercise。在英式英語，我們還可以說 get exercise。

★ 實用例句齊來學

- Lily never **does** any **exercise**. 莉莉從不做運動。
- Do you **take** enough **exercise**? 你有做足夠的運動嗎？
- He's lazy, and he doesn't **get** much **exercise**.
  他很懶惰，很少做運動。

💡 字詞搭配加分站

light exercise 輕度運動
- You may begin with **light exercise**. 你可以先做輕度運動。

vigorous exercise 劇烈運動
- You should avoid **vigorous exercise** after the operation.
  手術後，你應該避免做劇烈運動。

regular exercise 定期運動
- The doctor recommends **regular exercise**. 醫生建議定期做運動。

🔍 增潤知識大放送

在以上例子，exercise 作不可數名詞用。作可數名詞 exercises 用時，解作「一套運動或訓練動作」，例如：
- Let's do some **stretching exercises** first.
  我們先來做一些伸展運動吧。

exercise 本身也可作動詞用，解作「做運動」，例如：
- Did you **exercise** yesterday? 你昨天有做運動嗎？

漫畫看一看

This is the first time I've dived into the water.

Great! What did you see?

I saw a big group of clownfish!

Oh! You mean you saw a big school of clownfish? That's cool!

SCHOOL

字詞搭配你要知

🔊 地道英語這樣說

「一羣魚」不是 a group of fish。在這裏介紹兩個與魚類搭配的集合名詞（collective noun）。

第一個是 school，解作「魚羣」，與「學校」沒有半點關係。

第二個是 shoal，同樣解作「魚羣」，發音與 soul 相似，不過是以 sh 音開始，意思是「一大羣魚」。

⭐ 實用例句齊來學

- The swordfish will follow **a school of fish** for a long distance before it decides to attack.
  劍魚會跟蹤魚羣好一段距離，才加以攻擊。

- The sound of his music attracted **a school of dolphins**.
  他的樂聲引來一羣海豚。

- **A shoal of fish** jumps out of the sea. 一大羣魚跳出水面。

- **Shoals of** little **fish** were swimming around us.
  小魚成羣結隊在我們身邊游來游去。

👆 字詞搭配加分站

species of fish 魚的種類

- How many **species of fish** inhabit the waters in Hong Kong?
  香港水域棲息着多少種魚類？

catch a fish 捕魚

- He **caught** a big **fish**! 他捕捉了一條大魚！

🔍 增潤知識大放送

shoal 可引伸指「一大羣人」，通常作複數用，即 shoals，例如：

- **Shoals** of tourists visit the Disneyland in summer.
  夏天有大批遊客到訪迪士尼樂園。

✓ a bunch of flowers
✗ a bundle of flowers

漫畫看一看

🔊 地道英語這樣說

廣東話的「一紮花」和普通話的「一束花」,英文一般會用 a bunch of flowers 來表示。

而在一些特殊場合,如壽宴、婚宴等,我們多用 a bouquet of flowers 來表示「花束」。

⭐ 實用例句齊來學

- Dad gave mum **a huge bunch of flowers** for Valentine's Day.
  爸爸在情人節送了一大束花給媽媽。

- A fan rushed up on stage to give the singer **a bouquet of roses** during her concert last night.
  在昨晚的演唱會,一名歌迷衝到台上,向歌手獻上一束玫瑰花。

🔦 字詞搭配加分站

a mass of flowers 大量的花

- Look at **that mass of flowers** in the park! 看看公園裏的花海。

a carpet of flowers 滿地的花

- They made the hallway into **a carpet of flowers**.
  他們把走廊布置成一片花海。

🔍 增潤知識大放送

中文裏的「一束、一捆、一簇」都可以用 a bunch of 來表示,例如:a bunch of flowers / keys / grapes / carrots / bananas(一束花 / 一串鑰匙 / 一串葡萄 / 一束胡蘿蔔 / 一把香蕉)。

其實 bundle 也有「束」的意思,我們可以說 a bundle of sticks(一捆樹枝)、a thick bundle of clothes(一捆衣服),但不會說 a bundle of flowers。

✓ **make friends**
✗ **find friends**

漫畫看一看

If you go to the party, you'll find a lot of friends there.

Really? I've lost touch with some very good old school friends. Do you think I can find Lory there?

I guess he means you'll make a lot of friends there.

Yes, you're right. Let's go to the party and make new friends.

字詞搭配你要知

◀)) 地道英語這樣說

「結識朋友」不能説成 find a friend，因為 find a friend 指「把朋友找出來」。

「結識朋友」最常用的説法是 make friends，後面可加前置詞 with，表示交友的對象。

★ 實用例句齊來學

- His family moved a lot, and it wasn't easy to **make friends**.
  他一家屢次搬家，所以很難結識朋友。

- The children soon **made friends** with the kids next door.
  孩子很快就和鄰居的小孩成為了朋友。

字詞搭配加分站

become friends 成為朋友

- They met at a drawing class and **became friends**.
  他們在繪畫班認識，然後成為了朋友。

best friend 最好的朋友

- Tom is my **best friend**.
  湯姆是我最好的朋友。

win friends 贏得友誼

- How do we **win friends** easily?
  如何容易贏得友誼？

◎ 增潤知識大放送

口語裏，fall in with 和 get in with 也有「交朋友」的意思，但是這兩個説法一般帶有負面意思，例如：

- She's **fallen / got in with** a group of boys I don't like very much.
  她跟一羣我不喜歡的男孩混在一起。

漫畫看一看

He's very active. He sets up friendships with many people.

What do you mean?

Oops, I mean he makes friends with a lot of people.

That's good. It's always good to build friendships with others.

字詞搭配你要知 ✏️

🔊 地道英語這樣說

要表達「和某人建立友誼」，我們不會說 set up a friendship，而是說 make / form / build / develop a friendship。

⭐ 實用例句齊來學

- She has **built / formed** close **friendships** with her classmates.
  她和同學建立起深厚的友誼。

- He finds it difficult to **make / develop** lasting **friendships**.
  他覺得很難建立持久的友誼。

🔔 字詞搭配加分站

cherish a friendship 珍視友誼

- I **cherish** your **friendship** above anything else.
  我把你的友誼看得比什麼都重。

cultivate a friendship 培養友誼

- **Friendships** need time to **cultivate**. 友誼需要時間來培養。

end / break up a friendship 終止友誼

- You just can't walk away. It's no good to **end / break up a friendship** like that. 你不能一走了之，這樣斷絕來往並不好。

🔍 增潤知識大放送

friendship 既是可數名詞，又是不可數名詞。

和 friendship 搭配的前置詞以 with、between 或 among 居多，例如：

- I had no close **friendships with** other boys at school.
  我和校內其他男生沒有深厚的友誼。

- His visit to her studio led to a **friendship between** the two artists. 他到訪她的畫室，造就兩位藝術家成為了朋友。

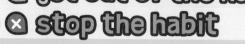

✓ get out of the habit
✗ stop the habit

漫畫看一看

Aunt Lily is worried about Uncle Tom because he's unable to stop the habit of smoking.

You mean he can't get out of the habit of smoking?

Yes.

Smoking is really a hard habit to break. The longer you smoke, the harder it is for you to quit.

🔊 地道英語這樣說

stop 不與 habit 搭配,例如我們可以用 stop smoking 來表達「戒煙」,但不能説 stop the habit of smoking。

如果要表達「改掉某習慣」,則可以用 get out of / break (oneself of) a habit。在俗語,也可以説 kick the habit。

⭐ 實用例句齊來學

- I **got out of the habit** of going to bed late.
  我改掉了晚睡的習慣。

- You must **break yourself of** this bad **habit**.
  你必須改掉這個壞習慣。

- Some smokers use hypnosis to help **kick the habit**.
  有些煙民透過催眠來戒煙。

🔔 字詞搭配加分站

become a habit 變成習慣

- Don't let playing on your phone **become a habit**.
  不要養成滑手機的習慣。

form a habit 養成習慣

- Try to **form** a good **habit** and eat healthily.
  盡量養成好習慣,健康飲食。

🔍 增潤知識大放送

我們也可用 give up、quit 來指戒掉習慣,但不須與 habit 搭配,例如:

- He **gave up** smoking three years ago. 他三年前戒煙了。

- If you've smoked for a long time, it can be very difficult to **quit**.
  長期吸煙的人不容易戒煙。

59

✓ suffer from a headache
✗ feel a headache

漫畫看一看

I felt a little headache.

What?

I mean I suffer from a mild headache. I feel unwell.

You poor thing — you need to take more rest.

字詞搭配你要知

🔊 地道英語這樣說

中文裏，我們會説「感到頭痛」，但英文並沒有 feel a headache 這個説法。我們一般會説 have / get a headache，當中的動詞 have 和 get 不能由 feel 取代。

其他可以搭配的動詞還有 suffer from、develop 和 experience。

⭐ 實用例句齊來學

- When I woke up, I **had** a serious **headache**.
  我起牀時感到劇烈頭痛。

- She **got a stomachache** and was absent from class today.
  她胃痛，今天缺席。

- Uncle Tom **developed** a severe **backache**.
  湯姆叔叔背部痛得很嚴重。

- Aunt Lily **suffers from** a terrible **toothache**.
  莉莉姨姨牙痛得很厲害。

💡 字詞搭配加分站

give someone a headache 引起頭痛
- Red wines **give** him **a headache**. 他喝紅酒會頭痛。

bad / severe / terrible headache 嚴重的頭痛
- Mum often has a **bad / severe / terrible headache** when the weather changes. 天氣轉時，媽媽頭痛得厲害。

🔍 增潤知識大放送

feel 可用於以下情況來表示身體不適，例如：

- John **felt sick** after eating the cake. 約翰吃了蛋糕後感到不適。

- If you **feel unwell**, take a rest first.
  如果你覺得身體不適，就先休息一下吧。

漫畫看一看

Have you given your homework yet?

To whom?

Oh, I mean if you have given in your homework.

Not yet. I'm still working on it. I think I'll hand it in tomorrow morning.

字詞搭配你要知

🔊 地道英語這樣說

如要表示「交功課」，搭配 homework 的動詞會是 hand in 或 give in，兩者皆指「提交、交上」，作及物動詞用，後接賓語。

⭐ 實用例句齊來學

- I want you to **hand in** this **homework** by next Monday.
  我希望你在下星期一前交功課。

- **Homework handed in** late will not be accepted.
  功課必須準時遞交。

- **Give** your **homework in** to the teacher when you have finished.
  做完功課後，請交給老師。

💣 字詞搭配加分站

for homework 功課是⋯⋯

- We have to write a 300-word composition **for homework** today.
  我們今天的功課是寫一篇 300 字的文章。

homework on 關於⋯⋯的功課

- I've got some **homework** to do **on** air pollution.
  我有些關於空氣污染的功課要做。

🔍 增潤知識大放送

homework 是不可數名詞，例如我們不能說 I have got many homework to do on History. 量詞 many 改為 a lot of 才正確，即是 I have got a lot of homework to do on History.（我有很多歷史功課要做。）

如果要量化 homework，就必須加上量詞 piece，例如：

- three **pieces** of **homework** 三份功課

✓ dark horse
✗ black horse

字詞搭配你要知

🔊 地道英語這樣說

英語中的 black horse，所指的是黑色的馬匹而已。

那些賽前被視為「冷門」而最後勝出的人，不叫 black horse，而叫 dark horse。

★ 實用例句齊來學

- He was regarded as a **dark horse** for the championship.
  他被視為冠軍黑馬。

- As a **dark horse** in the election, she did not receive massive recognition from the public.
  她是競選中的黑馬，未獲大多數公眾肯定。

💬 字詞搭配加分站

dark horse candidate 黑馬人選

- The **dark horse candidate** crowned Miss Hong Kong.
  黑馬人選榮獲香港小姐后冠。

🔍 增潤知識大放送

在英式英語，dark horse 也指「深藏不露或實力鮮為人知的人」，特別指具有別人意想不到的才華，卻不刻意顯露的人，例如：

- I never know what she's thinking – she's such a **dark horse**.
  我從來不知道她在想什麼——她是那種不露聲色的人。

相反地，fancied horse 和 fancied candidate 分別指「受人追捧的馬匹」和「獲看好的人選」，即「熱門（馬匹、人選）」，例如：

- He is the most **fancied candidate** for the election.
  他是選舉中最被看好的候選人。

✓ improve your English
✗ improve your English level

漫畫看一看

Miss, I want to improve my English level. What should I do?

First of all, you need to develop a sense of language.

What's it? And how?

For example, we say "improve your English"; we don't say "improve your English level". Understand?

Improve your English level

字詞搭配你要知

🔊 地道英語這樣說

「提高英語水平」正確的英文說法是 improve your English，level 一詞是多餘的。

同樣道理，我們會說 improve your tennis / Japanese（提高你的網球技藝 / 日語水平），但不說 improve your tennis level / Japanese level，因為前者已包含「提高……水平」的意思。

⭐ 實用例句齊來學

- This is a course for students who wish to **improve** their **English**.
  這門課為希望提高英語水平的學生而開設。

- I thought the best way to **improve** my **badminton** is to practice more. 我認為提高羽毛球技藝的最好辦法是多練習。

- In order to win, we need to **improve** our **performance**.
  如要勝出，我們必須提升我們的表現。

💡 字詞搭配加分站

improve rapidly 迅速提高
- He has **improved** his writing skills **rapidly**.
  他的寫作水平迅速提高了。

🔍 增潤知識大放送

在上述例子，improve 作及物動詞用，後接賓語，如 English、badminton 等。improve 也可作不及物動詞用，在這個情況，要表達相同的意思時，便要在後面加上 in，例如：

- He has **improved in** English. 他的英語水平提高了。

我們甚至可以反過來說 His English is improving.（他的英語水平正在提高。）

✅ gain knowledge
❌ learn knowledge

漫畫看一看

Cluck cluck. Nice to meet you! Do you understand me?

Cluck cluck. Absolutely! Did you learn the knowledge of our language?

Yes. I gain knowledge very easily.

Splendid! Can you share your knowledge with me?

字詞搭配你要知

🔊 地道英語這樣說

learn 是「學習」，knowledge 是「知識」，但 learn 和 knowledge 加起來並不是「學習知識」，因為英語不存在 learn knowledge 這個搭配。如果想説「學會了某些知識」，我們可以説 gain / acquire knowledge。

⭐ 實用例句齊來學

- The task gave me the chance to gain new knowledge.
  這項任務可以讓我學習新知識。

- He acquired some basic knowledge of the alien's language.
  他對外星人的語言有基本了解。

🔦 字詞搭配加分站

broad / wide knowledge 廣博的知識
- His knowledge of music is broad / wide. 他的音樂知識很廣泛。

limited knowledge 有限的知識
- We only have a limited knowledge of Metaverse.
  我們對元宇宙所知有限。

spread knowledge 傳播知識
- The Internet helps spread knowledge to people all over the world. 互聯網有助把知識傳播到世界各地的人。

🔍 增潤知識大放送

knowledge 是可以「吸收」的。在這個意義上，knowledge 可與 absorb 或 soak in 連用，例如：

- This smart kid can absorb / soak in knowledge quickly.
  這個聰明的小孩能夠快速吸收知識。

✓ sore leg
✗ painful leg

漫畫看一看

My legs are painful.

Are you hurt? Or did you twist your ankle?

No! I am saying my legs feel really sore after all the walking.

Oh, I see. Let's do some cool-down stretches.

字詞搭配你要知

🔊 地道英語這樣說

英語一般用形容詞 sore（疼痛的）或動詞 ache（疼痛），來形容「腿很痠痛」。如果說 painful legs，痛苦的程度會比較嚴重，例如腳跟扭傷了。只是單純痠痛的話，用 sore 和 aching 就行了。

⭐ 實用例句齊來學

- My **legs** are so **sore** after running. 跑步後，我的腿好痠痛。
- His **legs** are still **sore** from the surgery.
  他雙腿動了手術，仍然有些痛。
- How do I get my **legs** to stop **aching**? 如何讓我的腿不再痠痛？

💥 字詞搭配加分站

tired leg 疲憊的腿
- He crossed the finish line on **tired legs**.
  他拖着疲憊的雙腿越過終點。

injured leg 受傷的腿
- The dog has an **injured leg**. I think it was broken.
  那隻狗的腿受傷了，我猜是斷了。

shaky leg 顫抖的腿
- She rose to her feet on **shaky legs**. 她站起身來，雙腿發顫。

🔍 增潤知識大放送

sore 也可用來形容身體其他地方的疼痛，例如：
- My **eyes** feel really **sore**. 我雙眼很痛。
- I've got a **sore throat**. 我喉嚨痛。

ache 通常用於複合名詞，如 headache（頭痛）、stomachache（胃痛）、backache（背痛）等。

✓ full marks
✗ maximum marks

字詞搭配你要知

🔊 地道英語這樣說

mark 可以是成績的分數或等級，也可以用來評定操行或工作表現。成績或評價好，可以用 good 或 high 來搭配 mark。考獲最高分或滿分，則可用 top 或 full。

★ 實用例句齊來學

- He got **good marks** in Maths. 他數學科獲得好成績。
- The **highest mark** in the test was 93.
  這次測驗的最好成績是 93 分。
- You got **full marks** for getting the right answers.
  你答對所有題目，獲得滿分。
- I will give him **top marks** for honesty. 我對他的誠實要給予滿分。

💬 字詞搭配加分站

lower marks 成績或評價（比以前）差
- Her **marks** have been a lot **lower** this term.
  她這個學期的成績比以前差了很多。

poor marks 成績或評價差
- John got very **poor marks** in writing. 約翰寫作成績很差。

🔍 增潤知識大放送

英語不用 maximum marks 來指「滿分」，但 maximum 可用於以下情況：
- He obtained 82 **marks** out of a **maximum** of 100.
  滿分為 100 分，他獲得 82 分。

mark 是英式英語，美式英語一般用 grade 來表示成績的等級，例如：
- He got excellent **grades** in his exams. 他考試成績優異。

73

✔ make a mistake
✘ do a mistake

字詞搭配你要知

🔊 地道英語這樣說

在英語,「做錯事、犯錯了」不能說成 do a mistake,而是 make / commit a mistake。在口語,可以說 go wrong 或 get it wrong。

⭐ 實用例句齊來學

- I'm sorry, I **made a mistake**. 對不起,我犯錯了。
- Don't worry – everyone **commits mistakes**. 別擔心,人誰無過。
- The sum hasn't worked out, but I can't see where I **went wrong**. 總數算不出來,但我不明白錯在哪裏。
- Once again, you've **got it wrong**. 你又一再出錯了。

💡 字詞搭配加分站

admit a mistake 承認錯誤
- Did he **admit** his **mistakes**? 他肯認錯嗎?

correct a mistake 改正錯誤
- Can you help me **correct** my spelling **mistakes**? 你可以幫忙改正我的拼寫錯誤嗎?

learn from a mistake 從錯誤中吸取教訓
- All men make mistakes, but only wise men **learn from** their **mistakes**.
  任何人都會犯錯,但只有聰明的人才會從錯誤中吸取教訓。

🔍 增潤知識大放送

make 和 mistake 之間可以加入形容詞或修飾語來豐富詞義,例如:
- Alfie was playing badly, **making a lot of mistakes**.
  艾夫演 / 彈 / 打 / 踢得很差勁,出了很多錯。
- You have **made several grammatical mistakes**.
  你有幾處文法上的錯誤。

字詞搭配你要知

🔊 地道英語這樣說

「我感到高興」是 I am happy.「我感到累了」是 I'm tired. 但「我感到痛楚」卻不是 I am painful. 因為 painful 的主語往往不是人，而是傷口或人體的某個部位。

除此之外，painful 也可以解作「使人痛苦、疼痛或討厭的」，所以主語甚至可以是物件。

★ 實用例句齊來學

- Does the **cut** still feel **painful**? 傷口仍覺得痛嗎？
- My **boots** are **painful**. 靴子夾得我的腳很痛。
- The **lessons** are **painful**. 那些教訓很慘痛。

💡 字詞搭配加分站

slightly painful 有點痛苦
- These bruises can be **slightly painful**. 這些瘀傷會有一點點痛。

particularly painful 特別痛苦
- His failure in the exam was **particularly painful** to him.
  考試不及格對他來說尤其痛苦。

painful memories 痛苦的回憶
- These old photos brought back **painful memories**.
  這些舊照片喚起了痛苦的回憶。

🔍 增潤知識大放送

如果想要表達「我覺得痛楚」，我們可以說 I feel great pain. / I'm in a lot of pain.

英語口語中，動詞 kill 可用來指「疼痛」，例如：
- My legs are **killing** me. 我的腳痛得要命。

✓ throw a party
✗ open a party

漫畫看一看

We'll open a party this Sunday.

Are there many doors or windows in the party for you to open?

No. Why?

Are you saying you're going to throw a party on Sunday?

Yes, that's right.

字詞搭配你要知

🔊 地道英語這樣說

中文的「開」和英語的 open，在字詞搭配上有很大的分別。如果是「開電器」，我們會説 turn on 或 switch on。如果是「開派對」，最常見的説法是 have / give / throw a party。

⭐ 實用例句齊來學

- Let's **have a party** next weekend. 我們下周末開派對吧。
- On moving in they **gave** a huge housewarming **party**.
  他們一搬進來，就舉行了盛大的喬遷派對。
- They **threw a party** for Sarah's tenth birthday.
  他們舉辦了派對，慶祝莎拉十歲生日。

💡 字詞搭配加分站

organise a party 籌辦派對
- Have you ever **organised a party** for more than a hundred guests? 你有沒有試過籌辦一個來賓超過一百人的派對？

go to a party 參加派對
- Are you **going to the party**? 你會參加派對嗎？

invite someone to a paty 邀請某人參加派對
- Let's **invite** our teachers **to our party**.
  我們邀請老師來參加我們的派對吧。

🔍 增潤知識大放送

party 種類繁多，例如：birthday party（生日會）、Christmas party（聖誕聯歡會）、farewell party（歡送會）、dinner party（晚宴）、fancy-dress party [英式英語] / costume party [美式英語]（化妝舞會）。

✓ answer a phone
✗ receive a phone

字詞搭配你要知

◀)) 地道英語這樣說

中文裏的「接」，不能隨意翻譯成 receive。最常用來表示「接聽電話」的説法是 get the phone [口語] 和 answer the phone。而 lift the phone 或 pick up the phone 也包含同樣意思。

★ 實用例句齊來學

- Can you **get the phone**? 你能接電話嗎？
- I called several times but nobody **answered the phone**. 我打了幾次電話，但沒人接聽。
- She **lifted the phone** and said hello. 她拿起電話說你好。

字詞搭配加分站

on the phone 通話中
- Dad is **on the phone** at the moment. 爸爸正在通電話。

hang up the phone 掛斷電話
- I **hung up the phone** when she started shouting at me. 她開始對我大喊大叫時，我就把電話掛斷了。

be wanted on the phone 有電話找（某人）
- Mum, you **are wanted on the phone**! 媽媽，有電話找你。

○ 增潤知識大放送

英語中，我們其實可以説 receive a phone *call*，例如：
- I **received a phone *call*** from someone claiming to be from FBI. 有個自稱是美國聯邦調查局的人打電話給我。

lift the phone 或 pick up the phone 指「提起電話」這個動作，可指接電話或打電話，例如：
- She **lifted / picked up the phone** and dialed 999. 她拿起電話撥 999。

✓ take a plane
✗ ride on a plane

字詞搭配你要知

🔊 地道英語這樣說

「坐飛機」可以說 take / get a plane，而不能說 ride on a plane。要表達相同意思，還有很多說法，例如：take a flight、go by air、(go) by plane 或簡單一個動詞 fly。

⭐ 實用例句齊來學

- We **took a plane / flight** from Hong Kong to New York.
  我們坐飛機從香港去紐約。

- We **went by air / plane**. 我們是坐飛機去的。

- It's quicker **by plane**. 坐飛機快一些。

- Dad never liked **flying**. 爸爸從來都不喜歡坐飛機。

🔖 字詞搭配加分站

miss a plane 錯過航班

- If you hadn't been late, we wouldn't have **missed the plane**.
  如果不是你遲到，我們就不會錯過航班。

board / get on a plane 上飛機

- Everyone **boarded / got on a plane** and found their seats.
  所有人都登機了，也找到了自己的座位。

get off a plane 下飛機

- They looked tired when they **got off the plane**.
  他們下飛機時看來很疲倦。

🔍 增潤知識大放送

我們也可說 fly / travel in an aeroplane 來指「坐飛機」，例如：

- We didn't have much time, so we decided to **fly / travel in an aeroplane**. 我們不夠時間，所以決定坐飛機。

aeroplane 是英式英語的拼寫，airplane 則是美式英語的拼寫。

✅ good price
❌ suitable price

漫畫看一看

Do you want to buy it?

Yes, I like it a lot. And the price is suitable for me.

Do you mean the cap suits you and the price is good?

Yes. Thanks for correcting my mistakes.

字詞搭配你要知

◀)) 地道英語這樣說

我們可以說 I am suitable for the job. （我適合做那份工作。）
或 This book is suitable for self-study. （這本書適合自學。）
但是 suitable 不能與 price 搭配，不能說 The price is suitable for me.

要表達「價錢合理」，常用的字詞搭配有 good / right / fair price。

★ 實用例句齊來學

- I managed to get a **good price** for my old PC.
  我成功把舊電腦賣了一個好價錢。

- We sell quality kitchenware at the **right price**.
  我們出售價錢合理、品質優良的廚具。

- I think $100 is a **fair price** for a set of building blocks.
  我認為 100 元是一套積木套裝的合理價錢。

字詞搭配加分站

attractive price 價錢吸引

- They offer a good range of red wines at **attractive prices**.
  他們出售琳琅滿目而價錢吸引的紅酒。

steep price 價格過分昂貴

- The shoes look nice, but its **price** is a little **steep**.
  這雙鞋子看來不錯，但價格高得有點離譜。

🔍 增潤知識大放送

形容詞 reasonable 也可以指「價錢公道」，它可單獨使用，不一定與 price 搭配，例如：

- Apples are quite **reasonable** this week.
  這個星期蘋果的價格相當公道。

✓ low price
✗ cheap price

漫畫看一看

字詞搭配你要知

🔊 地道英語這樣說

price（價格）不能與 cheap（便宜的）或 expensive（昂貴的）搭配，而是用 low（低的）或 high（高的）來形容。而 salary（薪水）、wages（工資）、charge（收費）、cost（成本）、payment（報酬）、tax（稅）等，也是與 low 或 high 搭配。

⭐ 實用例句齊來學

- Well, the **price** is very **low**. Let's buy it.
  嗯，這個價格很低，買下來吧。

- Share **prices** reached an all-time **high** yesterday.
  股票價格昨天達到前所未有的最高點。

💡 字詞搭配加分站

reasonable price 合理的價格

- This restaurant serves good food at **reasonable prices**.
  這間餐廳提供價錢合理的美食。

economical 價格實惠的

- Only $50? That sounds **economical**.
  只需 50 元？聽起來很經濟實惠。

🔍 增潤知識大放送

如要表示「價廉物美」，我們可以說 It's a good buy. / It's a very good deal. / It's really good value for money.

形容詞 cheap 已有 low in price（價格低）的意思，所以再搭配 price 便是多餘。

cheap 也可用來形容商品和服務，例如：cheap furniture（平價家具）、cheap ticket（廉價票）、cheap fare（便宜的交通費）等。

字詞搭配你要知

🔊 地道英語這樣說

appear 的確有「出現」的意思,但值得注意的是,appear 一般指實質的事物,為人所看見的。

要表示抽象的事物,例如:problem(問題)、difficulty(困難)、opportunity(機會)、need(需要)等,則用 arise。

⭐ 實用例句齊來學

- Some unexpected **problems have arisen**.
  一些意想不到的問題出現了。

- Let's consider what kind of **difficulties** might **arise** from the situation. 我們研究一下在這個情況下會出現什麼困難。

- The bank will extend your loan, should the **need arise**.
  如有需要,銀行會延長你的貸款期。

👆 字詞搭配加分站

cause a problem 造成問題
- His rudeness could **cause problems**. 他態度惡劣,這會造成問題。

develop a problem 出現問題
- He **developed** a drinking **problem** after the death of his wife.
  妻子死後,他開始酗酒。

🔍 增潤知識大放送

arise 是正式用詞,多用於書面語,常用來表示突發或意外的事情。

在日常生活中,人們一般說 come up,比較通俗的說法是 crop up,例如:

- I have to go home early – something's **come up**.
  我要早點回家,突然發生了一些事。

- All sorts of difficulties **cropped up**. 各種困難接踵而來。

✔ cure a problem
✘ improve a problem

漫畫看一看

Breathe some fresh air. It's good for your lungs.

Wow, the air is so fresh!

Yes, the problem of air pollution has been improved a lot.

I guess you're saying the problem of air pollution has been cured. Right?

Yeap!

字詞搭配你要知

◀)) 地道英語這樣說

improve 指「改善；改進（某事情）」，即 to make something better。

中文可以說「改善一個問題」，但英文不能說 improve a problem，因為 to make a problem better 是說不通的。我們可以用動詞 solve、resolve、settle（解決）或 cure（矯正）來搭配 problem。

★ 實用例句齊來學

* Money cannot **solve / resolve / settle** their **problems**.
  錢不能解決他們的問題。

* If your computer stops working, re-booting might **cure the problem**. 要是電腦停止運作，不妨重新開機，問題或可解決。

字詞搭配加分站

run into a problem 遇到問題

* If you should ever **run into a problem** with your PC, we're here to help. 如果你的電腦出現問題，我們會隨時為你提供協助。

tackle / sort out / deal with a problem 處理問題

* The government is serious about **tackling / sorting out / dealing with the problem** of water pollution. 政府嚴肅處理海水污染問題。

🔍 增潤知識大放送

要表達口語的語氣，可用 sort out 和 put right，例如：

* I'm afraid I can't help you until I've **sorted** my own **problems out**.
  我連自己的問題還沒解決好前，恐怕幫不到你。

* If there's bullying in the classroom, it's the teacher who should **put the problem right**.
  如果班裏有學生被欺負，老師該有責任解決問題。

✓ make progress
✗ obtain progress

字詞搭配你要知

🔊 地道英語這樣說

事情有進展時，我們會說 make / achieve progress，而不說 obtain progress。

★ 實用例句齊來學

- Grandma is still in hospital, but she's **making** good **progress**.
  外婆還在醫院，但她康復得很快。

- In the last decade, China has **achieved** notable **progress** in its space programme.
  過去十年，中國在航天發展取得顯著成就。

💣 字詞搭配加分站

block progress 阻礙進展

- She is talented, but her sickness is **blocking** her **progress**.
  她很有才華，但是病情妨礙了她發展。

accelerate progress 加快進度

- They decided to **accelerate** the production **progress**.
  他們決定加快生產進度。

🔍 增潤知識大放送

progress 是不可數名詞，沒有複數形式，例如我們不能說 He is not making many progresses with Mandarin. 而是應該說 He is not making much progress with Mandarin.（他的普通話沒多大進步。）

progress 除了指抽象事情的「進度、進展」外，也指實際事物的「速度」，例如用於船隻航行上：

- The ship **made** slow **progress** through the rough sea.
  船在大風大浪中行駛得很慢。

漫畫看一看

Let's play a puzzle together!

What's the point of throwing the puzzle all over the place?

Silly me! I mean let's do a puzzle together.

Sure! I'm so good at it.

🔊 地道英語這樣說

puzzle 可以指「智力拼圖」，即 jigsaw puzzle，也可指「縱橫字謎」，即 crossword puzzle。

無論是 jigsaw puzzle 還是 crossword puzzle，中文都可以說「玩拼圖」或「玩縱橫字謎」，但英文不能用 play，而需用 do、put together、piece together、solve 等動詞來搭配。

⭐ 實用例句齊來學

- Let's **do a puzzle** together. 我們一起玩拼圖吧。

- It took me one whole week to **put together** a 1,000-piece **puzzle**. 我足足花了一個星期來完成這個 1,000 塊拼圖。

- Can you **piece the puzzle together**? 你能夠把這塊拼圖砌好嗎？

- She knows how to **solve a crossword puzzle** quickly. 她有辦法在短時間內完成縱橫字謎。

💬 字詞搭配加分站

piece of puzzle 拼圖的一塊

- A **piece of puzzle** is missing. Where is it? 有一塊拼圖不見了，它在哪裏呢？

complete a puzzle 完成拼圖／字謎

- We are only allowed 30 minutes to **complete this puzzle**. 我們只有 30 鐘來完成這個拼圖／字謎。

🔍 增潤知識大放送

puzzle 也可指「難題」或「令人費解的情況」，例如：

- Historians have been trying to solve this **puzzle** for years. 多年來，歷史學家一直試圖解開這個謎團。

✓ a large quantity
✗ a big quantity

漫畫看一看

SUPERMA

Why do these people rush to the store?

They want to stock up on food before the storm comes.

MILK

No need to rush. There's a big quantity of food out there.

You should say "a large quantity" instead.

字詞搭配你要知

🔊 地道英語這樣說

用英文表達「大量」時，千萬不要說 a big quantity。人們一般用形容詞 large、great、huge、vast 來搭配 quantity，以表示很大的數量。

⭐ 實用例句齊來學

- He has consumed **a large / great quantity** of alcohol.
  他攝取了大量酒精。

- **Huge quantities** of oil have spilt into the sea.
  大量石油已溢進海中。

- This software can handle **vast quantities** of data.
  這個軟件可處理大量資料。

💡 字詞搭配加分站

enormous quantity 龐大的數量

- Now they can produce the vaccine in **enormous quantities**.
  目前他們可以生產大量疫苗。

in quanity 大量地

- There's a discount for goods bought **in quantity**.
  大量購買商品可獲折扣優惠。

increasing quantity 不斷增長的數量

- An **increasing quantity** of cars is made in China.
  越來越多汽車在中國生產。

🔍 增潤知識大放送

反過來說，「少量」則是 a small / tiny / minute quantity。例如：

- Police found **a tiny quantity** of drugs in his car.
  警方在他的車輛發現了少量毒品。

字詞搭配你要知

◀)) 地道英語這樣說

big 與 rain 無法搭配，所以「大雨」不能説成 big rain。
我們一般用 heavy 來形容 rain，即 heavy rain。

此外，rain 是不可數名詞，我們不能説 a rain。

★ 實用例句齊來學

- We had **heavy rain** the whole morning. 整個上午都下大雨。

- The roads were flooded after the **heavy rain**.
  大雨過後，道路都被淹沒了。

字詞搭配加分站

light rain 細雨
- The weather forecast is for wind and **light rain**.
  天氣預報有風和細雨。

pouring / soaking rain 傾盆大雨
- **Pouring / soaking rain** drenched me. 傾盆大雨將我淋成落湯雞。

pour down（大雨）傾盆而下
- The rain **poured down** all afternoon. 傾盆大雨下了整整一個下午。

○ 增潤知識大放送

rain 可作動詞用，這時候必須和副詞 heavily 或 hard 搭配，
以表示「大雨」，例如：

- The roads flood whenever it **rains heavily**.
  一下大雨，道路就灌滿了水。

- It **rained hard** all day. 下了一整天大雨。

英語諺語 to rain cats and dogs 指「傾盆大雨」，例如：

- It's **raining cats and dogs** out there so I am soaked.
  外面傾盆大雨，我全身都濕透了。

✓ completely recover
✗ totally recover

漫畫看一看

字詞搭配你要知

◄)) 地道英語這樣說

驟眼看，I've totally recovered. 語法正確，但問題出在詞語搭配上。我們偶然還會聽到外國人這樣說，但那是極少數。

如要表示「完全康復過來」，fully recovered 是最常見的搭配。除此之外，還可以説 completely recovered。

★ 實用例句齊來學

- The doctor advises me to stay at home until I'm **fully recovered**.
  醫生勸我待在家裏，直到完全康復。

- He's lucky. He's **completely recovered** from the illness.
  他很幸運，已經完全康復過來。

🔔 字詞搭配加分站

recover from 從……康復過來

- He's **recovering from** a heart attack. 他心臟病發作，正在康復中。

gradually recover 逐漸恢復

- She needs time to **gradually recover** from the shock.
  她需要時間逐漸從那次打擊中恢復過來。

🔍 增潤知識大放送

換個角度，我們可把動詞 recover 轉成名詞 recovery 來用，例如：

- She made a speedy **recovery** from her stroke.
  她中風之後，康復進度迅速。

recover 或 recovery 是比較正式的説法。在日常生活中，人們會説 get over 或 shake off，例如：

- I've had a nasty cold, but I'm **getting over** it now.
  我得了重感冒，不過現在已經好過來了。

- It seems to be taking me a long time to **shake off** this cold.
  我似乎會花很多時間，才能把感冒醫好。

✓ work out a schedule
✗ arrange a schedule

漫畫看一看

They'll arrange a schedule for our holiday. I feel so relaxed.

I don't understand.

Why?

Do you mean they will help arrange our holiday and work out a schedule for us?

Holiday

Yes, yes!

字詞搭配你要知

🔊 地道英語這樣說

arrange 指「安排；籌劃」，已有 make plans for（計劃）的意思，所以再說 arrange a plan / schedule 便是多餘。

如要表示「訂出日程表」，正確的說法是 draw up / work out / make up / make out a schedule。

★ 實用例句齊來學

- Let's **work out** a study **schedule** by five.
  我們在五點前把溫習進度表訂出來吧。

- I've **drawn up** a tentative **schedule**, and we'll work out the details later.
  我已經初步把日程表擬訂好了，稍後我們會把細節訂出來。

💡 字詞搭配加分站

on schedule 準時

- They arrived **on schedule** at nine o'clock.
  他們準時在九點鐘到達。

ahead of schedule 早於原訂計劃

- We finished our work **ahead of schedule**.
  我們提前把工作完成。

behind schedule 遲於原訂計劃

- Due to the bad weather, the building work was **behind schedule**.
  由於天氣惡劣，建築工程趕不上原訂計劃。

🔍 增潤知識大放送

我們還可以說 arrange a meeting（安排會議）、arrange a trip（安排旅行）、arrange an appointment（安排會面）等。

✓ fasten a seat belt
✗ tie up a seat belt

字詞搭配你要知

🔊 地道英語這樣說

tie up 指「捆綁」，例如：tie the parcel up（把包裹捆綁起來）。因此，「繫好安全帶」不能説成 tie up a seat belt。

如要表示上述意思，我們一般用 do up、fasten、put on、wear 等來搭配 seat belt 或 safety belt。

★ 實用例句齊來學

- Don't forget to **do up** your **seat belt**. 不要忘記繫上安全帶。

- **Fasten** your **seat belt** during landing and take-off.
  飛機起飛和降落時，請繫好安全帶。

- He forgot to **put on** his **seat belt**. 他忘了繫上安全帶。

- It is compulsory to **wear a seat belt** when you are driving.
  開車時必須繫上安全帶。

💡 字詞搭配加分站

take off / undo / unfasten a seat belt 鬆開安全帶

- Can you please help me **take off / undo / unfasten** my **seat belt**? 你可以幫我把安全帶鬆開嗎？

🔍 增潤知識大放送

buckle 或 buckle up 是美式説法，同樣解作「繫上安全帶」，例如：

- We have **buckled (up)** our **seat belts** tightly.
  我們已把安全帶繫緊了。

buckle up 或 belt up 可作不及物動詞用，後面無須接賓語 seat belt，例如：

- Please **buckle up / belt up** so our flight can begin.
  請繫好安全帶，我們要起飛了。

✓ shoelaces are loose
✗ shoelaces are loosened

漫畫看一看

Your shoelaces are loosened.

Do you mean my shoelaces are loose? Yes, they are. I myself loosened them.

Why did you loosen them? It can be dangerous.

The shoes are too tight. They're hurting my feet.

🔊 地道英語這樣說

loosen 的確有「鬆開」的意思，但是「鞋帶鬆了」不能說成 The shoelaces are loosened. 因為 loosen 的主語必須是人，而鞋帶是死物。

如要表示「（某物）未繫上或鬆開的」，可用形容詞 loose、undone 或 untied。

★ 實用例句齊來學

- How come when I run or jog my **shoelaces** always get **loose**?
  為什麼我跑步時鞋帶總會鬆掉？
- Your **shoelaces** are **untied**. 你的鞋帶沒有繫好。
- My **shoelaces** came **undone** and I nearly tripped.
  鞋帶鬆開了，我差點兒絆倒。

💡 字詞搭配加分站

do up / tie shoelaces 繫鞋帶
- The little boy doesn't know how to **do up / tie** his **shoelaces**.
  那個小男孩不懂得綁鞋帶。

undo / untie shoelaces 解開鞋帶
- He never **undoes / unties** his **shoelaces** when he takes his shoes off. 他脫鞋時從來都不解開鞋帶。

🔍 增潤知識大放送

loose 也可形容其他事物，例如：a loose button（未釘牢的鈕釦）、 a loose tooth（鬆動的牙齒）。

loosen 作及物動詞用時，指「使……鬆開」，一般加上人物作主語，例如：
- Can you **loosen** the lid of this jar? 你能打開這個瓶蓋嗎？

✓ go to bed late
✗ sleep late

漫畫看一看

字詞搭配你要知

🔊 地道英語這樣說

sleep late 的意思是「睡到很晚才起牀」，例如：

- Let them **sleep late** on Saturday morning if they want to.
  星期六早上，他們想睡懶覺的話，就讓他們睡吧。

如要表示「很晚才睡」，一般說 go to bed late 或 be late going to bed。片語動詞 stay up（late）也有「深夜不睡」的意思。

★ 實用例句齊來學

- I **went to bed late** last night. 我昨晚很晚才睡。
- David **is** always **late going to bed**. 大衛經常很晚才睡。
- We **stayed up** till midnight yesterday. 我們昨晚熬到深夜才睡。
- Lily **stayed up late** to watch TV last night so she feels very tired now. 莉莉昨晚熬夜看電視，所以她現在覺得很累。

💡 字詞搭配加分站

cannot / be unable to sleep 不能入睡

- She **couldn't / was unable to sleep** so she got up to watch TV.
  她睡不着，所以起身看電視。

sleep through the night 一覺睡到天亮

- Very few babies **sleep through the night**. 很少嬰兒一覺睡到天亮。

sleep well / soundly 睡得好

- Were you **sleeping well / soundly** last night? 你昨晚睡得好嗎？

🔍 增潤知識大放送

英文俗語 night owl 指「晚睡的人」，即中文的「夜貓子」。owl（貓頭鷹）是晝伏夜出的動物，所以人們經常拿來比喻晚睡的人，例如：

- He's a **night owl**. He usually stays up late and feels most awake in the evening. 他是夜貓子，經常熬夜，傍晚時分特別清醒。

字詞搭配你要知

🔊 地道英語這樣說

食量大的人，可以說作 a big eater；揮霍無度的人，可以說作 a big spender；但煙癮大的人不能說成 a big smoker，而是 a heavy smoker。同樣，一個酒癮大的人是 a heavy drinker。

⭐ 實用例句齊來學

- Uncle Sam is a **heavy smoker**. He smokes more than 20 cigarettes a day.
  山姆叔叔的煙癮很大，他一天抽 20 多支煙。

- She's not a **heavy drinker**, but she drinks a lot whenever she feels stressed.
  她不是酒癮大的人，但每當她感到壓力就會痛飲一番。

🔦 字詞搭配加分站

light smoker 煙癮淺的人

- Before he quit smoking, he was just a **light smoker**.
  他戒煙前不過是一個煙癮很淺的人。

second-hand smoker 二手煙民

- **Second-hand smokers** may also develop lung cancer.
  二手煙民也有機會患上肺癌。

chain smoker 一支接一支吸煙的人

- How many cigarettes does a **chain smoker** smoke a day?
  煙不離手的人一天會抽多少支煙？

🔍 增潤知識大放送

heavy 是程度強烈的形容詞，有「大量；嚴重」之意，除了用來形容根深蒂固的習慣，還可來形容雨、雪或交通，例如：heavy rain（大雨）、heavy snow（大雪）、heavy traffic（擠擁的交通）。

✅ eat soup
❌ drink soup

字詞搭配你要知

🔊 地道英語這樣說

中國人喜歡喝湯，所以容易説出 drink soup 這樣的話。而在英文，「喝湯」的常用動詞是 eat，而不是 drink。

中湯講究清涼而不渾濁，所以能喝，西湯則較濃稠，加入了肉、菜或豆等食材，這類濃湯需要咀嚼，不能直接喝進口中。

⭐ 實用例句齊來學

- It's very cold. Let's **eat** some hot **soup** to warm up the body.
  天氣很冷，我們喝點熱湯暖暖身子吧。
- My children like **eating** tomato **soup** / borscht.
  我的孩子喜歡喝番茄湯 / 羅宋湯。

💡 字詞搭配加分站

cook / make soup 煮湯
- This chef **cooks** / **makes** the best chicken **soup** in town.
  這位廚師烹煮出城鎮裏最美味的雞湯。

ladle out soup 倒湯
- Mum **ladled out** three bowls of **soup**. 媽媽舀了三碗湯。

serve soup 端上湯
- The waiter **served** the **soup** first. 侍應先把湯端上。

bolt soup 匆匆嚥下湯
- Don't **bolt** the **soup** like that! 別那樣狼吞虎嚥地喝湯！

🔍 增潤知識大放送

有詞典專家曾説明過 eat 和 drink 的用法：如果是用勺子把湯從碗舀出來，就使用 eat；如果把碗端起來，直接用嘴喝，那就用 drink。為了避免混肴，我們可以用 have，例如：

- Let's **have** some **soup**. 我們喝湯吧。

✓ pack your suitcase
✗ pack up your suitcase

漫畫看一看

Have you packed up your suitcase yet?

What? I did pack up my job.

Oh, I'm sorry. I mean have you packed your suitcase?

Yes, I have. I'll leave tonight. I'm excited about the vacation.

字詞搭配你要知

🔊 地道英語這樣說

收拾行李，英文的說法是 pack your suitcase。這裏的 pack 作及物動詞用，後接賓語 suitcase。

pack 也可作不及物動詞，同樣包含「收拾行李」的意思，所以我們甚至可以省去 suitcase。

請注意 pack 後面不用加上 up。pack up 解作「停止」，例如 pack up smoking 等於「不再吸煙」，和「收拾行李」沒有半點關係。

★ 實用例句齊來學

- I'm leaving tomorrow, but I haven't packed my suitcase.
  我明天就走了，可是我還未收拾行李。
- We leave this evening, but I haven't begun to pack yet!
  我們今晚就走了，但我還未開始收拾行李！

💡 字詞搭配加分站

unpack a suitcase 把東西從行李拿出來
- Have you unpacked your suitcase yet?
  你還沒有把東西從行李拿出來嗎？

drag / pull a suitcase 拖行李
- The woman was dragging / pulling a very heavy suitcase.
  那個女人拖着一件很重的行李。

🔍 增潤知識大放送

時間充裕的話，我們會整齊地把衣服等東西放進行李，但對於一些大忙人，他們可能會匆匆把物品塞進行李，英文可說成 cram / stuff / throw something in the suitcase，例如：

- She stuffed a few clothes in the suitcase, grabbed her wallet and left. 她把幾件衣服塞進行李，拿起錢包就離開了。

✔ black tea
✘ red tea

漫畫看一看

My dad has a cup of red tea every morning.

Oh, I've never had a red tea before. Where did your dad get it?

Here it is. You can buy it everywhere.

Oh, no! This is black tea!

字詞搭配你要知

🔊 地道英語這樣說

綠茶是 green tea，但是紅茶不是 red tea，而是 black tea。據稱源於 18 世紀，福建武夷紅茶流入歐洲，因為茶葉顏色黑，英國人以貌取名，把它說成 black tea，而 red tea 只是「紅茶」的誤譯。

⭐ 實用例句齊來學

- Generally, **black tea** is stronger than green tea.
  一般來說，紅茶比綠茶濃。

- She drinks at least three cups of **black tea** per day.
  她每天至少喝三杯紅茶。

💡 字詞搭配加分站

brew / make tea 泡茶
- I'll **brew / make** some **tea** for you. 我來給你泡茶。

pour tea 倒茶
- **Pour** me a cup of **tea**, please. 請給我倒一杯茶。

steaming tea 熱騰騰的茶
- The waiter brought us a **steaming** pot of Dragon Well **tea**.
  侍應為我們送來了一壺熱騰騰的龍井茶。

sip tea 小口地呷茶
- He **sipped** his hot **tea** slowly. 他慢慢地呷熱茶。

🔍 增潤知識大放送

「濃茶」在英語中的說法不是 thick tea，而是 strong tea，例如：
- A cup of **strong tea** keeps me awake. 一杯濃茶讓我精神奕奕。

tea 一般作不可數名詞用，但表示茶的種類或數量時，可作可數名詞，例如：
- The restaurant offers a selection of herbal **teas**.
  餐廳提供多種草本茶。

✓ have a great time
✗ spend a great time

漫畫看一看

We all spent a great time at the party. Thank you!

You guys had a great time and enjoyed yourselves, didn't you?

Yes, we did.

That's good. It's about time to go home. Let's spend the rest of the weekend with your family.

字詞搭配你要知

◀)) 地道英語這樣說

我們對別人說 have a good / great time，意思等於 enjoy yourself，即是「玩得開心些」。當中 have 一詞表示「時間過得怎樣」，不能由 spend 取代。

★ 實用例句齊來學

- We all **had a good time**. 我們都玩得很開心。

- If you joined the Kung Fu club, don't expect to **have** an easy **time**. 你要是參加功夫學會，就別想會過得輕鬆。

- We **had the time of our lives**. / We **enjoyed ourselves** greatly. 我們玩得快活極了。

字詞搭配加分站

waste time 浪費時間

- Stop **wasting time**. We have to finish this today. 別再浪費時間了，我們要在今天之內把它完成。

kill time 消磨時間

- We **killed time** watching the TV. 我們看電視來消磨時間。

◯ 增潤知識大放送

spend time 所強調的是如何利用時間，例如：

- You should **spend** more **time** practicing oral English. 你應多花些時間練習英文口語。

spend 可後接與時間有關的名詞或名詞片語，例如：

- We **spent a pleasant hour or two** playing in the park. 我們在公園裏愉快地度過了一兩個小時。

- She **spent a year** in Beijing learning Mandarin. 她用了一年時間在北京學普通話。

56

漫畫看一看

Can you recommend some tourist places to us?

You want to visit the tourist spots?

There're many attractions here. You may go to the Peak. It's a very beautiful scenic spot.

Thank you. That sounds very nice.

字詞搭配你要知

🔊 地道英語這樣說

tourist 指「遊客」。至於「旅遊景點」，可有不同的叫法，最常見的是 tourist attraction / sight / spot。而 tourist place 這個說法十分奇怪，也不自然。

★ 實用例句齊來學

- Ngong Ping Village has become a major **tourist attraction** in Hong Kong.
  昂平市集已成為香港一個主要的旅遊景點。

- The Peak is one of Hong Kong's most popular **tourist sights**.
  山頂是香港熱門的旅遊景點之一。

- This little old town is famous for its many **tourist spots**.
  這個古老的小鎮有很多遊覽勝地，十分有名。

📢 字詞搭配加分站

tourist destination 旅遊目的地 / 勝地

- Can you name the top ten **tourist destinations** in the world?
  你能說出全球十大旅遊勝地嗎？

draw / attract tourists 吸引遊客

- How to **draw** / **attract** more **tourists** to Hong Kong?
  如何吸引更多遊客來香港？

🔍 增潤知識大放送

強調名勝風景美好時，可用 scenic spot / location。scenic 一詞有「風景優美、景物怡人」的意思。例如：

- There are many **scenic spots** in Beijing.
  北京有不少風景遊覽點。

- That is a nice **scenic location** for a picnic.
  那裏風景優美，是個野餐的好地點。

57

漫畫看一看

At this time of the day the roads are always crowded with people.

Yes, this is the rush hour and the traffic is very crowded, too.

Do you mean the traffic is heavy?

Ahem, yes. Look! The cars are stuck.

It's sad that we can't fly.

字詞搭配你要知

🔊 地道英語這樣說

crowded 大多用於形容有形的空間，例如：a crowded room（擠擁的房間）、a crowded bus（擠擁的巴士）、a shop crowded with shoppers（擠滿了顧客的商店）。如想表達「交通繁忙、擠擁」，我們一般用 busy 和 heavy。

★ 實用例句齊來學

- The **traffic** is very **heavy** this time of the day.
  每天這個時候交通都很擠擁。

- The food delivery motorcyclist weaved his way through the **busy traffic**. 電單車外賣速遞員在擠擁的車流中迂迴穿行。

字詞搭配加分站

traffic builds up... 交通開始繁忙

- In Central, **traffic** was already **building up** as early as 3 p.m.
  中環的交通在下午 3 點就開始繁忙了。

traffic thickens... 交通擠擁起來

- **Traffic thickens** noticeably after 5 p.m.
  下午 5 點以後，交通明顯擠擁起來。

traffic clogs... 交通堵塞

- **Traffic clogs** the main streets in Causeway Bay.
  交通堵塞了銅鑼灣的主要街道。

🔍 增潤知識大放送

traffic 與名詞搭配來表示「交通擠擁」的例子有 traffic jam / congestion，例如：

- We were stuck in a **traffic jam** for almost two hours.
  我們塞車塞了近兩小時。

漫畫看一看

字詞搭配你要知

🔊 地道英語這樣說

「我贏了你」不能説成 I won you. 因為 win 後面只接事物和事件，例如：competition（比賽）、battle（戰役）、election（選舉）、prize（獎品）、medal（獎牌），甚或 friendship（友情）。

如果想説「贏了某人、擊敗某對手」，我們用 beat 或 defeat。

⭐ 實用例句齊來學

- We **beat** their team with a score of 4-3.
  我們以四比三的分數擊敗了他們那隊。

- I **beat** the other player by four points.
  我以四分的優勢擊敗了對手。

- Our team **was defeated by** three goals to one.
  我們這隊以一比三被擊敗。

💡 字詞搭配加分站

win comfortably 輕鬆獲勝

- We **won** the competition **comfortably**.
  我們輕鬆贏得比賽。

win narrowly 險勝

- She **narrowly won** the first round of the election.
  她在首輪競選中險勝。

🔍 增潤知識大放送

win 也可作不及物動詞用，例如：

- I've **won** (the game)!
  我贏了比賽！

- They didn't deserve to **win** – they played badly.
  他們不配獲勝——他們打得太差勁了。

✓ strong wind
✗ big wind

漫畫看一看

字詞搭配你要知

🔊 地道英語這樣說

「大雨」不是 big rain，而是 heavy rain；「大風」也不是 big wind，而是 strong wind。另外，我們也可以用 fierce、harsh、high、stiff 等形容詞來搭配 wind，以表示「大風」或「狂風」。

★ 實用例句齊來學

- Wear a windbreaker – the **wind** is **strong** out there.
  穿上風衣吧，外面風很大。
- Rain and **high winds** are forecast. 天氣預報說有雨和大風。
- A **fierce wind** swept through the city. 狂風席捲了整個城市。

💥 字詞搭配加分站

warm wind 暖風
- The **wind** is so **warm** today. 今天的風很暖和。

icy wind 寒風
- Fans braved **icy winds** to cheer on their team.
  球迷頂着寒風給他們支持的球隊吶喊加油。

bitter wind 刺骨的寒風
- The **bitter wind** cut right through us. 刺骨的寒風把我們冷透了。

wind roars 狂風咆哮
- The **wind roared** through the tunnel like thunder.
  狂風如雷鳴般呼嘯着穿過隧道。

🔍 增潤知識大放送

同樣道理，「微風」不能説成 small wind，恰當的形容詞包括 light、slight、moderate 等，例如：
- There is a **light wind** blowing. 微風輕拂。
- A **slight wind** stirred amidst the trees. 微風吹過樹梢。

✓ a pack of wolves
✗ a group of wolves

字詞搭配你要知

🔊 地道英語這樣說

在英語，「一羣狼」該説成 a pack of wolves。pack 是個集合名詞，特別用於一羣獵食的動物，可以是狼羣、狗羣等。

除此之外，「羊羣」不要説成 a group of sheep，而是説 a flock of sheep。

⭐ 實用例句齊來學

- The girl was chased by **a great pack of wolves**.
  那個女孩被一大羣狼追着。

- **A pack of fierce dogs** came swarming out of the door.
  一羣兇猛的狗從門口湧出來。

- In her dream, Angel was surrounded by **a pack of ravening wolves**. 在夢裏，安琪被一羣覓食的餓狼圍住。

💡 字詞搭配加分站

a herd of... 一羣（獸羣、牧羣）
- **a herd of** cattle / elephants / horses / deer 一羣牛 / 象 / 馬 / 鹿

a flock of... 一羣（羊）
- **a flock of** sheep / goats 一羣綿羊 / 山羊

a litter of... 一窩（幼小的動物）
- **a litter of** puppies / kittens / piglets 一窩小狗 / 小貓 / 小豬

🔍 增潤知識大放送

a flock of 也可用來指鳥類，例如：a flock of gulls / crows / doves（一羣海鷗 / 烏鴉 / 鴿子）。

表示「一羣獅子」時，我們會説 a pride of lions，例如：
- **A pride of lions** is hunting down a prey animal.
  一羣獅子成羣出動圍捕獵物。

練習室 1

Choose the correct verb for the following sentences.
Tick the correct box .

請為下列句子選出正確的動詞，並在 ☐ 加 ✔。

| 範例 | Let's (☐ A. open ✔ B. throw ☐ C. work) a party. |

1 The earthquake (☐ A. made ☐ B. did ☐ C. formed) widespread damage to the village.

2 I like to sit down and (☐ A. do ☐ B. play ☐ C. work out) the crossword.

3 I really enjoy (☐ A. doing ☐ B. having ☐ C. working) exercise every day.

4 Mary wants to (☐ A. take up ☐ B. study ☐ C. do) a course in Maths.

5 My father (☐ A. infects ☐ B. has ☐ C. catches) a backache so he couldn't sleep well.

6 Only 40% of the students who (☐ A. had ☐ B. joined ☐ C. took) the final exam passed it.

7 His misbehaviour has (☐ A. arisen ☐ B. caused ☐ C. appeared) us too many problems.

8 David seems to (☐ A. catch ☐ B. infect ☐ C. suffer) the flu every winter.

9 He fell asleep and (☐ A. made ☐ B. had ☐ C. thought) strange dreams.

10 He is a young man of (☐ A. big ☐ B. strong ☐ C. great) ability.

參考答案：1. B 2. A 3. A 4. C 5. B 6. C 7. B 8. A 9. B 10. C

練習室 2

What's the opposite of the following words in bold?
Write the answer in the spaces provided.

以下粗體字的相反詞是什麼？請在橫線上填寫答案。

例	There is a **light** wind blowing.	strong
	I **lost** the game.	_____
	Have you **unpacked** your suitcase yet?	_____
	She is a **heavy** smoker.	_____
	The little girl can **do up** her shoelaces.	_____
	Fasten your seat belt now.	_____
	Our work is **ahead of** schedule.	_____
	We had **heavy** rain the whole evening.	_____
	Hang up the phone.	_____
	Chloe got very **good** marks in reading.	_____
	He has a **broad** knowledge of world history.	_____

參考答案：1. won　2. packed　3. light　4. undo / untie　5. Unfasten / Take off / Undo　6. behind　7. light　8. pick up / get / answer / lift　9. poor　10. limited

Fill in the blanks with the correct preposition for the following sentences.

請為下列句子填寫正確的介詞。

| 範例 | Can you provide us ___with___ an example? |

1 No more play as we have to study _____ the exams.

2 They met _____ some difficulties when doing the work.

3 We arrived _____ the airport in early morning.

4 David got _____ his bicycle and rode off.

5 Dad is suffering _____ a heavy cold.

6 We have just signed _____ for a course in drawing.

7 These words might sound difficult. You may look them _____ in a dictionary.

8 Students can buy books and stationery _____ a discount.

9 When I got in, a wild dog barked _____ me.

10 Let me walk you _____. I'll show you to the door.

參考答案：1. for 2. with 3. at 4. on 5. from 6. up 7. up 8. at 9. at 10. out

練習室 4

Fill in the blanks with the correct quantifier for the following sentences.

請為下列句子填寫正確的量詞。

範例 There live a ___pack___ of wild dogs in the forest.

1 A _____ of little fish is swimming around us.

2 The monkey has eaten a whole _____ of bananas.

3 The bridegroom gave the bride a _____ of red roses.

4 The sheep were chased by a _____ of wild wolves.

5 There was a _____ of cattle on the farm.

6 We found a _____ of kittens among the leaves.

7 They kept a small _____ of sheep on the hill.

8 We have collected a large _____ of sticks.

9 How much is this _____ of grapes?

10 This picture shows a _____ of wild lions living in Africa.

參考答案：1. school 2. bunch 3. bunch / bouquet 4. pack 5. herd 6. litter 7. flock 8. bundle 9. bunch 10. pride

133

練習室 5

There is a mistake in each of the following sentences. Circle and correct them in the spaces provided.

下列句子均有一處錯誤，請圈起錯誤的部分，並在橫線上寫上正確答案。

範例	The film is a ⟨black⟩ horse for the award.	dark
1	The traffic is usually crowded in the morning.	_____
2	We spent the time of our lives. Thank you!	_____
3	Aunt Kelly drinks a cup of red tea every morning.	_____
4	It's freezing. Let's drink some hot soup.	_____
5	They are determined to improve the pollution problem.	_____
6	Grandma hasn't yet totally recovered from her illness.	_____
7	We consumed big quantities of food and drinks at the party.	_____
8	We slept late to watch the World Cup.	_____
9	I've to go now; some problems have just appeared.	_____
10	I'm not going to buy it. The price is very expensive.	_____

參考答案：1. crowded → heavy / busy 2. spent → had 3. red → black 4. drink → eat 5. improve → solve / resolve / settle / cure 6. totally → fully / completely 7. big → large / great → huge 8. slept → went to bed / stayed up 9. appeared → arisen / come up / cropped up 10. expensive → high

練習室 6

There is a mistake in each of the following sentences. Strike them through and correct them in the spaces provided.

下列句子均有一處錯誤，請刪去錯誤的部分，並在橫線上寫上正確答案。

例	She ~~felt~~ a little headache.	had
1	We are determination to reach our goals.	___
2	They met an accident in the mountains.	___
3	We're seeing our friends away at the airport.	___
4	Mary fell down her bike and hurt her leg.	___
5	"Wang, wang!" the dog went.	___
6	He raised an example to illustrate his point.	___
7	Friendships need time to set up.	___
8	He can't stop the habit of gambling.	___
9	I'm not getting much progress with my Mandarin.	___
10	Mr. Smith is a big smoker, so few people were surprised when he died of lung cancer.	___

參考答案：1. determination → determined 2. met → met with / had 3. away → off 4. down → o
5. Wang, wang → Woof, woof 6. raised → took / used / gave 7. set up → develop / c
8. stop → get out of / kick / break 9. getting → making / achieving 10. big → heavy

趣味漫畫學英語

小學漫畫英語王：Collocations 字詞搭配

作　　者：Aman Chiu
繪　　圖：黃裳
責任編輯：黃稔茵
美術設計：劉麗萍
出　　版：新雅文化事業有限公司
　　　　　香港英皇道 499 號北角工業大廈 18 樓
　　　　　電話：(852) 2138 7998
　　　　　傳真：(852) 2597 4003
　　　　　網址：http://www.sunya.com.hk
　　　　　電郵：marketing@sunya.com.hk
發　　行：香港聯合書刊物流有限公司
　　　　　香港荃灣德士古道 220-248 號荃灣工業中心 16 樓
　　　　　電話：(852) 2150 2100
　　　　　傳真：(852) 2407 3062
　　　　　電郵：info@suplogistics.com.hk
印　　刷：中華商務彩色印刷有限公司
　　　　　香港新界大埔汀麗路 36 號
版　　次：二〇二三年五月初版
　　　　　二〇二四年六月第二次印刷

ISBN: 978-962-08-8191-6